THE MIGHTY EXPLORERS

JoGenii

RED PANDA

BAL SIMHA
FINDS THE COURAGE

PURBA M.

Illustrated by
RAJDEEPA SEAL

For Jojo and Koko, the only critics I'm truly afraid of.

For Sid, my partner in every brave beginning.

Published by Red Panda, an imprint of Westland Books, a division of Nasadiya Technologies Private Limited, in 2026

No. 269/2B, First Floor, 'Irai Arul', Vimalraj Street, Nethaji Nagar, Alapakkam Main Road, Maduravoyal, Chennai 600095

Westland, the Westland logo, Red Panda and the Red Panda logo are the trademarks of Nasadiya Technologies Private Limited, or its affiliates.

ISBN: 9789379852076

10 9 8 7 6 5 4 3 2 1

Printed at Nutech Print Services Pvt. Ltd

Meet Bal Simha,
blessed by
Goddess Durga's light,
He is brave at heart
and gentle in might.

In Khojpur, where the gods' vahanas live and play,
Five super friends zoom around all day.
They are the Mighty Explorers of Khojpur—kind, brave and true.
Come join them, adventure awaits you.

Say hello to brave Bal Simha and wise Uluka Di,
Clever Nanha Mooshak and strong Veer Nandi,
Then there is the watchful Garuda Sen,
Together they all fly through sunshine and rain.

Now this is the story of Bal Simha, you see,
The bravest explorer, yet kind as can be.
His roar was loud, his mane shone bright,
His heart was gentle, his hugs warm and tight.

Bal Simha knew that he could be strong,
But the real joy is helping others along.

One sunny afternoon, warm and clear,
The Mighty Explorers played without a fear.
They built a bridge with sticks and stone,
Across a stream that gently flowed.

'Careful,' said Uluka Di, calm and slow,
'This bridge is new. Be careful, as you go.'

Crraaack! Suddenly, a stick gave way,
Nanha Mooshak gave a scared squeak right away.
He ran back but held on tight,
The water below shimmered bright.

'I'm scared,' said Nanha Mooshak, in a voice so frail,
'I don't know what to do, I might fail.'

Bal Simha's heart also beat fast and loud,
But he didn't growl or roar out aloud.
He knew his roar would cause a scare,
Nanha Mooshak needed gentle care.

Bal Simha took a breath, held his roar inside,
He stepped forward to be by Nanha Mooshak's side.
'Don't worry,' he said, soft and clear,
'I'm right here. You're safe, my dear.'

He lay down low, tail steady and still,
Making a bridge with courage and will.
Nanha Mooshak climbed across, taking small steps,
The Mighty Explorers watched with bated breath.

Everyone cheered—with smiles so warm,
'That was brave,' said Veer Nandi, strong and calm.

'You didn't scare or shout or fight,
You helped gently and that felt right.'

As they rested beneath a shady tree,
Uluka Di opened a book quietly.
'This reminds me,' she said with a
smile so bright,
'Of a story where courage chose
kindness over might.'

'Long ago,' Uluka Di read soft and slow,
'The world needed a guardian with a fearless glow.'
So Goddess Durga appeared, calm and bright,
With courage that cared, not with might.'

Durga did not roar to scare the land,
She stood to protect, with a gentle hand.
Where someone was afraid or felt small,
Her courage was like a strong wall.

She showed the world that valour can be,
Gentle and kind for all to see.

Uluka Di closed her book with grace.
Bal Simha smiled, lifting his face.
'So brave,' he said, with eyes kind,
'Is helping others feel safe inside.'

Khojpur felt warm and bright,
When courage chose care over fright.

It's good to be like Bal Simha, brave and kind,
Using your courage with heart and mind.
Being brave is not to scare or shout,
It's staying calm and helping out.

Stay close, be gentle, show your care.
That's true courage anywhere.
When strength protects with love and grace,
True courage shines upon your face.

ABOUT THE AUTHOR

Purba M. is a parent, storyteller and believer in compassionate parenting values.

Through her work with JoGenii, she creates story worlds and learning experiences that encourage kindness, courage and confidence in young children.

She believes that the bravest lessons are often the quietest ones—and that every child deserves stories that feel safe, warm and true.

ABOUT THE ILLUSTRATOR

With a love for colours and curiosity, **Rajdeepa Seal** brings stories to life. She enjoys creating playful, imaginative visuals that invite readers to explore and dream.

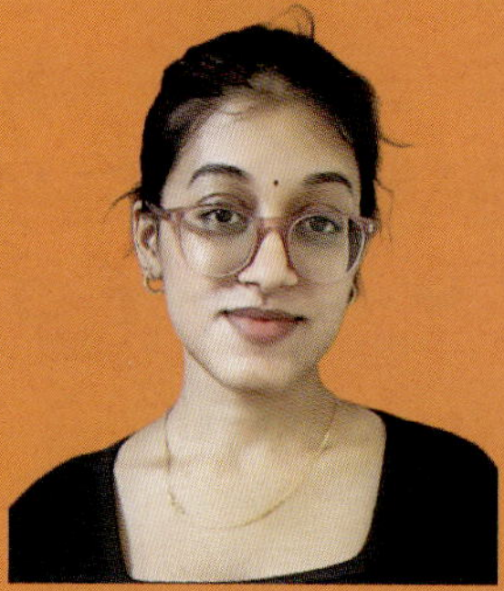

Find more about JoGenii here:
www.jogenii.com

See more of the Mighty Explorers here:
https://www.youtube.com/@JoGenii